PIRATES of the CARIBBEAN

JACK SPARROW

The Pirate Chase

by Rob Kidd
Illustrated by Jean-Paul Orpinas

Based on the earlier life of the character, Jack Sparrow,
created for the theatrical motion picture,
"Pirates of the Caribbean: The Curse of the Black Pearl"
Screen Story by Ted Elliott & Terry Rossio and Stuart Beattie and Jay Wolpert,
Screenplay by Ted Elliott & Terry Rossio,
and characters created for the theatrical motion pictures
"Pirates of the Caribbean: Dead Man's Chest" and
"Pirates of the Caribbean: At World's End"
written by Ted Elliott & Terry Rossio

DISNEY PRESS   Spotlight

visit us at www.abdopublishing.com

Reinforced library bound edition published in 2009 by Spotlight, a division of ABDO Publishing Group, 8000 West 78th Street, Edina, Minnesota 55439. This edition reprinted by arrangement with Hyperion Books for Children, an imprint of Disney Book Group, LLC. www.disneybooks.com

Library of Congress Cataloging-in-Publication Data

Kidd, Rob.
    Pirates of the Caribbean, Jack Sparrow / by Rob Kidd ; illustrated by Jean-Paul Orpinas. -- Reinforced library bound ed.
        v. cm.
    "Based on the earlier life of the character, Jack Sparrow, created for the theatrical motion picture, 'Pirates of the Caribbean: The Curse of the Black Pearl'. . . and characters created for the theatrical motion pictures 'Pirates of the Caribbean: Dead Man's Chest' and 'Pirates of the Caribbean 3.'"
    Contents: The coming storm -- The siren song -- The pirate chase -- The sword of Cortés -- The Age of Bronze -- Silver -- City of gold -- The timekeeper.
    ISBN 978-1-59961-525-7 (book 3: The pirate chase)
    I. Orpinas, Jean-Paul, ill. II. Pirates of the Caribbean, the curse of the Black Pearl (Motion picture) III. Pirates of the Caribbean, dead man's chest (Motion picture) IV. Pirates of the Caribbean, at world's end (Motion picture) V. Title.
    PZ7.K53148Pir 2008
    [Fic]--dc22

                                                                          2008000720

The Pirate Chase

Captain's Log:

Having recently defeated some most vicious (and most beautiful) mermaids—agents of the legendary Sirens—we set sail in the hope of finishing up our quest to procure the legendary Sword of Cortés, a sword with unimaginable power. Once the sheath and the sword are united, the power of the sword shoots from unimaginable to godlike. I expertly ascertained that the sheath belonging to that sword—a sheath which the crew of the mighty _Barnacle_ happens to currently possess—must be able to somehow lead us to the Sword itself. I gracefully set the sheath on the deck of our great ship, and it spun around like a compass needle, pointing toward an island very likely, in my opinion, to be Isla Fortuna. At least, in the general direction, no doubt. After all, how could an enchanted sheath steer us wrong? It won't be long before the Sword of Cortés is back in that sheath—and all of its power is in the hands of the mighty Captain ~~Ja~~ Barnacle's crew! Our only obstacle is the notorious, vicious pirate Left-Foot Louis. He should be an easy adversary to overcome, however, given our track record defeating roaring sea beasties and pirates who control storms.

CHAPTER ONE

"See, I told you!" Jack Sparrow proclaimed from the prow of the *Barnacle* as the misty green shape of an island became clear on the horizon. "The sheath's led us straight to Isla Fortuna." He bowed. "No applause necessary," he continued despite the fact that no one had clapped, "stow it till we have the Sword in hand."

Just days before, the sheath to the fabled Sword of Cortés had fallen to the deck of the

Barnacle and acted as a compass, pointing the crew somewhere. Jack guessed Isla Fortuna. Legend had it that once the Sword and sheath were united, the already powerful Sword would become invincible!

"Oh, come on, Jack. Ye're mad. Sure, the sheath has led us straight to an *island*," Arabella, Jack's trusted first mate said, folding her arms. The sea breeze tugged at her tousled auburn hair. "We don't yet know *which* island. And, if it *is* Isla Fortuna, how do we know the Sword is *there*?"

"You're splitting hairs, *chere*," said Jean, a young sailor that Jack's crew had picked up on Isla Esquelética, the very first island they visited on their adventure. Jean stood next to Jack at the very prow of the *Barnacle*, gazing at the island in the distance. Sea foam splashed at his feet.

"It doesn't matter if this is where the

Sword is. The sheath wants us to go to this island, so it has to be important for some reason, *non*?"

Jean's friend Tumen, an equally great sailor and expert navigator, who had also been rescued from Isla Esquelética by the *Barnacle*, added, "Jean is right. Where else could that sheath be leading us but somewhere related to the Sword?"

"Perhaps it is leading us to somewhere terrible," the aristocratic runaway Fitzwilliam P. Dalton III pointed out. "If the sheath really were cursed, it could be pointing us straight to our doom."

Some people just couldn't take an enchanted sheath pointing toward an island for the obvious stroke of good luck it was. Annoying, in Jack's opinion.

Jack stepped up and sighed. "You're all wrong. We *are* going the right way. We *are* about to find the Sword and, in the unlikely event that we are, in fact, headed into danger and not to the Sword itself, well, I say it's about time somebody—anybody—on this crew had a proper sense of adventure!"

Arabella sneered. "Trust me, Jack. Anybody who sails with ye is willing to take risks." Jack smiled proudly, "Why thank you, mate," he responded.

Jack took the ship's wheel firmly in hand and steered the *Barnacle* straight toward the island and whatever it held in store for the crew. With the wind snapping the sails and the *Barnacle* dancing on the waves, Jack thought he no doubt made a fine picture of a ship's captain—worthy of a painting.

Then, Jack stumbled as Constance, the ship's resident girl-turned-cat, wound herself around his ankles, her tail curling up his boot. "Jean, get this blasted cat—"

"My *sister!*" Jean snapped.

"—*the feline in question* off my boots," Jack said.

Jean shook his head, looking down fondly at the purring cat. Jean was the only one in the crew who was ever so adoring toward the ragged, ill-tempered beast. This made sense, as Jean insisted that the beast in question was his sister under a mystic's curse.

"I could pull her away," Jean said, shrugging, "but what good would it do? Soon she would return." Jean sighed. "I think she liiiiikes you," he said in a singsong tone to Jack, blowing mocking kisses at his captain.

Jack sneered back at Jean and his half-cat-sister-thing.

Within a few minutes, the island was close enough for the crew to make out details: the high mountains in the distance and the many palm trees on the coastline. Arabella grabbed Fitzwilliam's spyglass and surveyed the coastline.

"Jack, ye were right when ye guessed that the sheath was pointing to the Sword— whether this island be Isla Fortuna or not," Arabella said, her face as serious as Jack had ever seen it.

"Thank you," Jack said flatly, grabbing the spyglass from her and surveying the island himself. "And what, pray tell, finally convinced you of my great, underestimated wisdom?"

"Nothing. But now I believe in the sheath's magic. Because that—" She raised her hand to the horizon, her finger pointing at fluttering white outlines of sails. "—that is the *Cutlass*."

"Left-Foot Louis's ship?" Fitzwilliam said, leaning so far over the railing that he was in danger of falling overboard. Jack resisted the urge to boot Fitzwilliam in the aristocratic rear and help the process along. "How can you be certain?"

"See the flag? The skull and crossbones of the Jolly Roger are scarlet instead of white—that's him. That's his symbol." Arabella hugged herself, looking sad and uncomfortable.

Jack adjusted the spyglass to better see the *Cutlass*. Arabella's sharp eyes had not failed her. The blood-red skull appeared to be laughing eerily, as the flag flapped in the wind. A few figures moved about on deck—Louis's crew—all busy with something or other.

This was good news, as far as Jack was concerned. Left-Foot Louis was a notorious pirate. Evil and deranged—at best. But the crew also suspected that Louis had the powerful Sword of Cortés in his possession. And the crew wanted the Sword of Cortés badly—to keep its power out of the hands of pirates, and to experience the freedom that power would bring.

"Sails down," Jack commanded, tucking the spyglass into his belt so that he could steer the ship eastward. "We need to make ourselves a little less conspicuous."

Jean smirked. "I never thought I would hear you say you wanted to be less conspicuous, Jack."

"Okay then," Jack said, "why don't we just send up smoke signals, alert them to our presence and invite them aboard for high tea?"

Tumen and Jean nodded quickly and shuffled across the deck. They had crossed Louis once before. The pirate had sworn to kill them both—and skin Constance—

the next time around.* "No, there's really no need to see that brute or his crew again," Jean said.

"Aye, we'll see him again," Arabella said quietly. "But not until we're ready."

"I like your style," Jack said, winking at her.

Jack steered the *Barnacle* toward the island's main port, Puerto San Judas. The crew was tense as the *Barnacle* slipped away from the *Cutlass*, and even Jack felt a little stir of dread. Not that he couldn't lick Louis in a fair fight any day of the week, but the *Cutlass* had cannons. Large ones. Lots of them. The *Barnacle* was little more than a fishing boat. That sort of thing skewed the odds in Louis's favor.

As soon as they rounded the sandy cove of Isla Fortuna, and palm trees finally hid the

---

* As Jean and Tumen told the crew in Vol. 2: *The Siren Song*

Barnacle entirely, the crew breathed a collective sigh of relief. Jean and Tumen grinned at one another, and even Fitzwilliam's stiff spine seemed to relax a little.

Arabella was the one crew member who didn't relax. She stared into the swaying palms as though she could still see the scarlet skull of Louis's Jolly Roger. Jack wondered if she had somehow missed the part where he had cleverly steered them from danger.

"No use in worrying," Jack said. "We'll be docked in Puerto San Judas in no time."

"Food . . ." Jean said, his face lighting up with a dreamy smile. "Ah, if only we can find some good shrimp *etouffee*—"

"First, we find an inn," Tumen said, shifting his back. "This deck is hard. Beds are soft."

"No. First we speak to the local constabulary

about Louis." Fitzwilliam nodded vigorously and straightened his grand coat which, despite his numerous adventures, always seemed to be in pristine shape. "They cannot be aware that such a despicable character lingers so close to their town. For surely they would have taken steps to arrest him immediately."

Jack picked up Fitzwilliam's spyglass again to get a good look at Puerto San Judas, which was already taking shape on the far horizon of the island's cove. Then he lowered the spyglass and blinked hard. He looked again in disbelief. Finally, he handed the glass to Jean and said, "Tell me how many ships you see in the harbor."

Jean peered through the spyglass for a very long time before he answered. "None. So?"

Jack folded his arms. "Dunno, mate. It just seems odd that a port town on any island in the Caribbean would be free of ships."

"Isla Fortuna is a small island. Difficult to find," Jean pointed out. "Not everybody is as good at navigating as me and Tumen," he said proudly. "Maybe all the ships are lost out at sea looking for it."

"Then that makes us a touch above the rest, doesn't it?" Jack grinned. "Including especially this vessel's illustrious captain?"

"And let's not forget the sheath, which pointed us directly *to* this island," Arabella reminded the boys.

"Well," Jack said, quickly changing the subject, "if we're the only customers they've got, we can expect a king's welcome." With the *Cutlass* out of sight, he felt it safe to give his command: "Raise sails and pull into port!"

"Aye, aye!" Jean crowed, and he and Tumen set to work.

As the *Barnacle* docked, the kingly welcome didn't materialize. Not even a princely welcome. No welcome at all, if you wanted to be precise about it. Even as the crew tied the *Barnacle* to the pier, no one appeared to demand a fee, write down the crewmembers' names, or offer them wares.

Every dusty old road was completely deserted.

"This is too quiet," Jean said. Constance's gray fur stood on end, and she hissed at the silent town.

Arabella whispered, "Something terrible happened here. Louis—did he—"

Jack shook his head. "Hasn't been any kind of a fight, love. No broken windows, no bullet holes in the walls. No fires. Left-Foot Louis leaves his mark on a town, as Jean and Tumen can testify."

The two friends nodded uncomfortably in agreement.

"Look," Fitzwilliam said, pointing at a nearby shop. "The butcher—he is open for business. And the apothecary, too. Not a locked door in the place." Relieved, they all rushed toward the markets—but they were all empty of people. Yet the dairy offered fresh milk, the butcher's displayed recently sliced ham, and the fishmonger still had a barrelful of very fresh catfish flapping about, waiting to be sold.

"All these items had to be put out this morning," Jean said. "No earlier than that. But now, the people who set up these shops are nowhere to be found."

A shiver ran through Arabella. "It's as if they vanished, very suddenly, by a great force and without warning."

CHAPTER TWO

The crew wandered through the silent roads of Puerto San Judas, staring at the deserted shops and alleyways. None of them could quite believe their eyes. Arabella was right. It was as though every person who lived there had disappeared in an instant, leaving everything around them completely untouched. The whole town was snatched up—but how?

Jack glanced at the members of his crew, who all looked extremely uneasy. He needed to steady everyone's nerves, and fast.

"Nice and quiet here, isn't it?" Jack asked, realizing that perhaps his question wasn't the best solution to his crew's jitters.

"This must be a town of ghosts," Tumen replied. Arabella's eyes went wide. In the magically cursed Caribbean, a town of ghosts was not beyond comprehension.

It was Jean who snapped out of the frightened daze first. As the crew walked past an inn, Jean stood up straight and sniffed the air. Then he breathed out a long, loud sigh and began stumbling inside.

"Is he quite all right?" Fitzwilliam gaped at him. "He acts like a man possessed!"

"No one here is possessed!" Jack shouted dismissively, hoping to turn the conversation away from ghosts and demons.

But when the crew ran toward Jean, they quickly discovered that he *was* possessed, in a way. But it wasn't a mystical being that had done it . . . he was bending over a bubbling pot of deeply aromatic soup. "Gumbo!" he whispered, as reverent as a priest in church. "Seafood gumbo, just the way I like it. Ah, *c'est merveilleux!*"

"Ought to have known you'd lose your mind over food," Jack grumbled. Then he took a deep whiff of the spicy scent of the gumbo. At that moment, it occurred to him just how hungry he really was. "Don't suppose there's enough for all of us?"

"Most days, this would be enough for twice as many," Tumen declared, staring down into the pot. "Today, with five very hungry people—maybe *just* enough."

Arabella snatched the bowls from the shelves and began serving up helpings just as quickly as she used to pour grog at the Faithful Bride.

"There's even enough here for Constance, if she likes." Arabella said.

Constance had never been fond of Arabella, and this small offering didn't change that. The cat simply hissed at Arabella and jumped up on the bar near Jack, who had instantly gone to work on his bowl. Jean petted Constance's back and said apologetically, "Don't mind her. My sister was never big on gumbo. It was always steak tartare for her, or nothing at all!"

"And now she enjoys eating live mice," Jack muttered, slurping a spoonful of gumbo. "Quite the refined palate."

Constance's tail twitched. Hurriedly, Jean fed her a bit of crabmeat from his bowl, and that seemed to make her happy for the moment. In fact, during the few minutes it took them to eat their meal, all of them were happy—or, at least, so relieved to have good, warm food in their stomachs that they couldn't worry about any of the many other problems they had to worry about.

Jack looked mournfully at his empty bowl. "Can't you refill this for me, Arabella?"

"Is yer leg broken?" Arabella kept right on eating. "Fill yer bowl yerself."

Jack decided that though he was hungry, he wasn't hungry enough to serve himself. And already his mind was turning back to the difficulties of their situation. "Something's amiss in this town."

"Ye think so?" Arabella said sarcastically.

"He states the obvious," Fitzwilliam said, nodding. "Nevertheless, something extraordinarily odd has taken place here in Puerto San Judas."

Arabella folded her hands beneath her

chin, and began to muse. "The townsfolk could be in hiding from Louis. Even before the *Cutlass* sailed in, a lookout might've spotted his scarlet flag. If they saw that, they would have been frightened for sure—and with good reason."

Jean shook his head. "If they saw him so far away, they would have had time to prepare their escape. They'd have put out the fires in the stoves; taken meat, bread, and ale with them."

"So," Jack said, pacing up and down the tavern's dirty floor, "we find ourselves in a peculiar situation."

Tumen sighed. "As usual."

"I've never heard a sailor tell a story anything like this one. We have to find out what happened, and we can't do that unless we investigate," Arabella said decisively. "We should search the island. Spread out.

Someone must still be out there, and maybe that person could explain. If we break into groups, we could cover more ground—"

"Excuse me." Jack stood up, hitting the table and making the bowls and spoons clatter. "*I'm* the captain here. That means *I* make the plans."

"Captain? Ha!" Fitzwilliam scoffed.

Jack sneered and then continued, "So, here is what I command: We must find out what happened, and that means an investigation's in order. So we will search the island. Spread out. Find somebody who can explain. We should break into groups so we can cover more territory. Savvy?"

Tumen rolled his eyes. Jean shook his head wearily. Arabella crossed her arms, but she said only, "Well, Jack, I don't see how anyone could argue with such a sensible plan."

"Exactly." Jack grinned. "What say we start right away?"

They walked out into the empty and eerily quiet town square and split into groups. Jean and Tumen chose to go with one another, best friends that they were.

Fitzwilliam stepped up and said, "Arabella, I shall accompany you."

"And why is that?" Jack demanded to know.

"Why ever not?" Fitzwilliam countered.

This was an incredibly rude question, Jack thought, especially considering that he had no good answer for it. "Arabella ought to come with me. For protection," Jack finally said.

"I assure you that I am quite capable of protecting a lady," Fitzwilliam countered, his chest swelling up like a peacock's.

Arabella stepped between them. "I hate to

interrupt yer rare display of chivalry, but as it turns out, I can protect myself." She made her point by holding up a pistol. It looked comfortable in her hand.

Jack had forgotten she'd tucked that into her skirt pocket back in Tortuga, but he didn't feel better. "Right. Splendid. So then, Arabella, you can come with me for *my* protection. Being that you're the one who is carrying a firearm."

"Ah." Arabella laughed. "The thing's not even real." She bent the handle back and it opened, revealing hairpins and coins and that sort of thing. It was more a purse than a weapon. "It's a fancy little pillbox of sorts. I used it back at the Faithful Bride to scare away unwelcome customers," she explained. "Now," she continued, "we should break up into parties of two. Jack," she said, "ye clearly need no protection. Yer bloody well

capable of getting yerself out of a mess all
your own, as we've seen. So Fitz should walk
with me, because I have the means to protect
him," she said waving the pistol she hoped
would be convincing enough to scare away
any would-be attackers. Fitzwilliam looked
aghast. He began to open his mouth in
protest, but Arabella continued her lecture
to Jack. "Besides," she said, "ye already have
a companion."

"What?" Jack said. But then he looked
down to see Constance, still only inches
from his foot, blinking up at him with lov-
ing yellow eyes. Jack sighed. "Oh, great. I've
got the bloody cat."

Jean came to his side, and for one hopeful
moment Jack thought maybe he'd insist on
traveling with his "sister" himself. Instead
he whispered, "Jack, with Constance by
your side, you must be very careful!"

"Not to worry, mate." Jack stared pitifully at the cat. "Like Bell here said, I am at no risk of danger whatsoever. Savvy?"

"I'm not worried about *you*, Jack . . ." Jean bent down and stroked Constance's ears. "When Constance scratched Louis across the face, leaving the scars the pirate is now marked with, he vowed that the next time he saw her, he would skin her! So you must stay far from him, Jack."

"Yes, yes. Very well," Jack said dismissively. "Cat, Louis: keep away. Got it. Okay, crew, shall we be on our way now? We shall convene again in port alongside the *Barnacle* at high noon."

"Not long," Tumen pointed out, one hand toward the sky. He had learned back home how to tell the time by the sun's position. "Half an hour, no more."

Jack nodded. "Puerto San Judas is not

such a large town. Besides, the townsfolk didn't perform this cruel disappearing act more than a half hour ago. We can tell from the fresh things in the shops. If they're on foot, we'll find them by then. If not—we wouldn't find them in a century."

"High noon, then," Fitzwilliam said, squinting into the sun. "But what shall we do if one of our parties has not returned by that time?"

Silence befell the crew.

"Nonsense," Jack said. "The crew of the *Barnacle* is the most cunning in all the Caribbean. I will see you all here at noon, with or without the people of this island."

CHAPTER THREE

$\mathcal{I}$n the Caribbean, every saint's feast day was a reason for celebration—fine food, finer wine, and dancing into the night. As a rule, Jack was strongly in favor of feast days. So he knew that Dominic de Silos was the patron saint of mad dogs and pregnant women, Mary Magdalene the patron saint of apothecaries and hairdressers, and Jude—for whom this town had been named—was the patron saint of desperate situations.

Jack stood before the small wooden

church that had been built in honor of Saint Jude—who was also the patron saint of this town. A town full of desperate situations, Jack guessed, especially now that the towns-people had all vanished. The church stood on a small hill surrounded by sparse grass and at the foot of a long and winding crude dirt road.

"Impossible causes and desperate situations. So—that's your game, isn't it?" Jack said to the saint, or at any rate to the church the townsfolk had built in his honor.

Constance, who trotted along beside Jack's feet, mewed loudly, as if questioning him.

"Wasn't speaking to you, love," he snapped. The cat's mangy head drooped so sadly that Jack almost felt bad for her. Almost. Jack still thought Jean was bark-ing mad to believe that his sister had been transformed into a cat. But he had to admit, Constance behaved just like a girl. Temperamental, flirtatious, sometimes savage. With the cat, or sister, or whatever it was, Jack walked up to the doors of the Church of San Judas and stepped inside.

Like the rest of the town, the church appeared to have been recently—very recently—and very suddenly—abandoned. Candles flickered alongside each wall. Incense still burned on the altar, and the air was heavy and sweet with its scent. Shafts of sunlight were tinted blue and green and gold by the stained glass of the windows. Jack walked slowly up the aisle.

Constance mewed again, a tiny, frightened sound, and crept along a few paces behind Jack, looking over her shoulder every now and then to be sure they were alone.

Jack made his way toward the altar—then felt a soft breeze tickling his face. After another few steps he could see the source of the draft: a small door at the far corner of the church had been left open.

Then Jack heard a loud voice yell, "Dig faster, curs!"

Unless Jean or Tumen had suddenly grown up, Arabella had become a man, or Fitzwilliam had learned to swear loudly— which was the least likely of the three sce-narios—that voice didn't belong to anyone Jack knew.

He crept to the edge of the doorway and peered outside. Alongside the church was the town's small graveyard, and in this graveyard, two brawny men were digging. An even larger man stood nearby with his hands on his hips, watching them. Jack real-ized that they were unearthing a grave.

Then Jack realized something else, something far worse. The clothing these men wore—kerchiefs around their heads, swords at their sides, and bandoliers across their shoulders—didn't look like the kind of thing the friendly citizens of Puerto San Judas would be sporting.

"Pirates," Jack whispered to himself. No doubt these were crew members from the *Cutlass*, taking advantage of the deserted town to do some looting. Dirty, stinking, thieving cowards, the lot of them. Of course, Jack, too, was often dirty, occasionally *borrowed* useful items, and thought Arabella was a little too particular about body odor to ever be a true sailor. But he was no coward, and he was no pirate.

The two diggers cast aside their shovels, then began working with ropes, pulling hard—and lifting the coffin to the surface.

As the grimy lid appeared, the biggest pirate, who had his back to Jack, laughed loudly. "Pity that Francois never told me he had the parchment—"

One of the other pirates, panting from the effort of lifting the coffin, asked, "You wouldn't have killed him, then?"

"Are you mad?" the largest pirate boomed. "I'd have been even quicker in killing him. And then I'd search him thoroughly before I left his body behind. Might have gotten the parchment there and then."

Jack frowned, confused. A whole empty town, ripe for the picking—and the pirates were only after a scrap of parchment? When they could have stolen every bit of gold in Puerto San Judas—on all of Isla Fortuna, in fact—without any difficulty at all?

Then Jack realized that this parchment, whatever it might be, was important enough to have been buried with the man whose remains lay in that coffin.

The biggest pirate continued—more quietly, as if to himself—"I'll soon have the parchment back in my hands. Already got the Sword. Once I have the scabbard, the power of all the gods is mine!"

He had the Sword. He now had the parchment, too, whatever power that might hold. And now, he only needed the sheath. The large pirate could only be one man—Left-Foot Louis!

As the pirates pried off the lid of the coffin, Jack started to retreat. He needed to tell his crew he'd found Louis, and about this new development—the parchment. Jack stepped backwards carefully. But not carefully enough, and his foot came down hard onto Constance's tail.

The cat screeched an incredibly loud hiss

which echoed throughout the church. Jack jumped up, stumbling in a panic. He tried to think of a way to quiet the cat, but it was no use; Constance's yowl had already startled the pirates. One of them wheeled around, and Jack gaped as he locked eyes with Louis. The pirate had bright red hair, a gold tooth among his rotten set of choppers, and three pink scars scratched across his face—scars that looked as if they'd been left by a cat's claws.

"Well, well, well. What have we here?" Louis grinned. "Looks like that mangy cat that scratched my face. And she's brought along a mangy friend." His rotten, gold-toothed grin spread even wider. "So, tell me—which one of you will I be skinning first?"

"A charming invitation," Jack said, "but I fear we must decline. Pressing engagements elsewhere. Ta now." Jack ran as fast as he could toward the door at the other end of the church, Constance at his heels. But when Jack was just a few steps away, the front door swung open to reveal Left-Foot Louis's two men, each of them brandishing a dagger. Jack skidded to a stop against the church's planked wood floor, then he whirled around in the other direction—only to see Louis advancing down the aisle toward him.

The pirate's steps were awkward and strange. Jack realized that at least some of the outlandish stories were true; Left-Foot Louis really did have two left feet. They both turned toward the right, which gave him a limping gait. But that didn't slow him down much. In fact, as far as Jack could tell, it didn't slow him down at all.

This would be a marvelous time for one of my brilliant plans, Jack thought. *Ideal. Surely one will come along any second now. Any second. Surely.*

Constance cringed at Jack's feet, wrapping her tail around his ankles.

Louis cackled and drew a sword. And at that moment, any brilliant idea that might have been lurking in Jack's mind, waiting to hatch, was instantly obliterated. So did all the many ideas that weren't brilliant at all. *That's the Sword of Cortés!* Jack thought.

It was unmistakable. The markings on the jeweled hilt were an exact match to the scabbard! It could only be the Sword of Cortés. Only that sword would ever fit in the sheath Jack had found—the sheath that Louis was now staring at with the same disbelief that had Jack gaping at the Sword!

"What's this?" The pirate hooked his free hand into his belt and rocked back and forth in satisfaction. "Thought after retrieving the parchment, we'd have to go searching for the sheath for the Sword of Cortés. And now the scabbard's walked right in here on its own."

"Not quite," Jack retorted. "The sheath's not a free agent, you see. It walked in here with *me*, because it's *mine*."

Louis swung his blade once, getting ready for battle. "And you'll be leaving it to me in your will. They'll be reading that will of yours soon, probably in the next few moments actually. Then I'll have my sword, my sheath, and my parchment—and finally ultimate power, too, will be all mine."

Again with the parchment. Jack decided that the first thing he'd do after he quickly defeated Louis would be to find that parchment for himself. And then find out how it related to the Sword.

This was assuming, of course, that he survived.

CHAPTER FOUR

"Hello? Anyone?" Fitzwilliam called as he and Arabella walked down one of the dirt roads of Puerto San Judas. They had traveled halfway through the town already with no success, and to Fitzwilliam it seemed like time to start speaking up a bit.

"Are ye daft?" Arabella snapped, slapping Fitzwilliam upside the head. "Don't yell!"

"How else are we to summon those who might be in hiding?" Fitzwilliam asked.

"The townspeople aren't the only ones we

might wind up summoning. Pirates—or someone or something else responsible for whatever happened to the townspeople—well, they could hear ye, too."

Fitzwilliam straightened up. "Your reasoning is sound. I shall search more quietly."

Arabella shook her head. "Ye always talk so proper and politely. Even when we're wandering through a ghost town haunted by who knows what."

"That is how I was raised."

"Aye, I know. It just—it isn't much like the way sailors talk. Not the sailors I've known, at least," Arabella said.

Fitzwilliam looked past her to see if anyone might be lurking on the winding path that headed downhill, but it was empty. "I could never speak in any other manner to a lady," he said.

Arabella laughed. "Me? A lady? Ha!" She

gestured toward her tattered dress, which had been cheap and plain even when it was new, long ago. With one hand she brushed her messy auburn hair away from her face. "Be serious."

"I am always serious."

She considered this. "Aye, I'll not argue with ye there."

Fitzwilliam folded his hands behind his back. "My mother used to say that elegant dresses and stylish accoutrements do not a lady make. A true lady is known by her behavior—her intelligence, her dignity, and her thoughtfulness toward others. In that sense, I believe you are a fine lady indeed, Arabella."

"Well," Arabella looked away from him, as if searching for other villagers, but her cheeks were turning a little pink, "it sounds as though Lady Dalton was a very wise woman."

"She was," Fitzwilliam replied somberly, then decided it was best to tell the full truth. "Of course, she still insisted upon a new gown at least once a month."

They both laughed together, too amused to be afraid. So it was with no fear or expectations that Fitzwilliam peered around the next corner they came to, in order to get a glimpse down an empty alleyway.

But the alleyway wasn't empty at all.

"Aiiiigh!" shouted the man in the alley, throwing his arms up in the air in a fright. He had a curly golden beard that stood out in all directions from his chin. Several silver chains and a few coins fell from his hands. They clinked upon the rocky path as they fell.

"Hold there, pirate!" Fitzwilliam demanded.

"I'm no pirate!" the curly-bearded man shouted back. Then he added, with a grin,

"And you're no man, just a boy who can't make me do a thing."

"It's not the boys ye need fear," Arabella said, smiling and pulling her fake pistol from the pocket of her skirt. "So I suggest ye begin telling us what happened in Puerto San Judas. Right now."

Sheepishly, the man held up his hands. "It's nothing to do with me, that I promise you."

Fitzwilliam stepped forward. "And why should we believe the word of a pirate?"

"I told you, I'm no pirate!" he responded.

"Regardless, pirate, why should we believe such a tale?" Fitzwilliam said, folding his arms proudly. "You are the only one we have found on this island. And you are engaging in *thievery*."

But then Arabella said, "He's telling the truth. Look at his clothes. That jacket's never been soaked at sea, and his boots are too thin for any storm. No pirate—no honest *sailor* even—would ever be dressed that way."

"Still," Fitzwilliam continued, "you have not yet answered our question. What happened to the people here?"

The curly-bearded man hesitated. "No need to go waving guns about; we're friends here, ain't we?" he asked with a smarmy, unfriendly grin. "I'll say what I know, but it's not much. And I tell you now, you won't believe me."

"Try us." Arabella sighed, lowering her pistol. "I believe in all sorts of things I didn't believe in a month ago."

"Traveling with Jack Sparrow does have that effect," Fitzwilliam agreed.

The bearded man's eyes lit up with a slight shock at the mention of Jack's name, but he did not say why. Then he continued,

"Well, you see, I'm a businessman like any other—"

"You are a *thief*," Fitzwilliam interrupted, pointing to the loot that had fallen to the ground.

Grinning nervously, the curly-bearded man shrugged. "It's a living. But as I was saying, I was going about my daily work like anyone else this morning. 'Twas checking to see if the alehouse might have failed to lock the till. They do that sometimes, you know. In no fit shape when they close up for the night. Scandalous, what drink does to some folk—"

Arabella cleared her throat. "If ye could get back to the subject."

"Right. I was just about there when I hear the cry go up. 'Pirates!' The townsfolk were all yelling, screaming, scattering in every direction. I was ready to join them, too! But

wall in disappointment. "It was very special to me."

Arabella felt a pang of grief. She knew Fitzwilliam had lost his sister the same way Arabella had lost her mother—to pirates.

"I've dealt with his type more than ye have," Arabella said, "so I should've known he'd go for your golden watch." She bowed her head.

"Never mind," Fitzwilliam said suddenly, "it was only a thing. And things can be replaced and retrieved and bartered. At least neither one of us was hurt."

Arabella nodded. "All right, then," she said looking down the road. "That's the town mill, isn't it? A useful landmark, so let's remember it."

Fitzwilliam held up one hand. "Wait—Arabella, I believe I hear something. Perhaps it is the thief, and we can catch him after all!"

Hopeful, Arabella listened carefully; she heard something, too, but it made her gasp instead of smile. "That's more than one set of footsteps, Fitz. In fact, it's several people. All of them coming this way."

They looked at one another, then slowly peered around the nearest corner. Even at that angle, each of them got a good view of the shabby, sword-wielding figures running toward them through the brush.

"Pirates!" Fitzwilliam said.

Arabella dropped to the ground and pulled him down beside her. They both crouched on the ground, listening in horror to the sound of the pirates' footsteps coming closer. Arabella whispered in his ear, "If they find us, they'll kill us!"

She was trembling. Fitzwilliam had heard

that a gentleman should always comfort a lady in distress. "You cannot know that for certain."

Arabella wasn't comforted. As she stared into space, she said quietly, "Yes. I can."

CHAPTER FIVE

*J*ack had managed to leap out an open church window, and Constance followed close behind. They had run through the brush behind the church, but Louis and his thugs were hot on their trail. Jack held his sword-fighting skills in high esteem, but he could be realistic about his limitations when the situation called for it. And, at the moment, the situation was calling for it. Loudly.

"*Aha!*" Left-Foot Louis shouted, slashing

the Sword of Cortés straight toward Jack's head as he ran. Jack ducked—he was very good at ducking—but the blade still swung close enough to shear off a lock of his hair. This was getting serious.

Louis was fast, and his sword was enchanted with magical powers—maybe not godlike powers, not till it was reunited with its sheath—but magic all the same. Two other pirates were not far behind, ready to jump in if Jack should manage to get the upper hand. But it didn't look like Jack was ever going to get the upper hand.

If worse came to worst—and matters were headed in that general direction—Jack would be able to cast off in the *Barnacle*. Surely the others would be gathering back there by now. It seemed as though the chase had begun quite a while ago. The *Cutlass* might pursue them, but the pirate crew was probably spread out across Isla Fortuna. It would take time for Left-Foot Louis to get all of them back on board, time the *Barnacle* could use to escape.

Constance, her fur standing on end, was keeping pace beside Jack. She screeched as they both heard the shouts of the pirates behind them. Jack decided to risk a glance over his shoulder. Louis's crewmen were too close for comfort—only a couple of yards behind him and Constance, along with Left-Foot Louis himself. His awkward, rolling gait looked even stranger when he was running.

Jack began swerving and ducking wherever he could, Constance close behind. This alleyway, that winding path—Jack ran through empty shops and houses and did whatever he could think of to lose his pursuers, but it was no use. Then Jack had an idea: Louis was after the cat.

"Might want to make yourself scarce," Jack panted as he ran, speaking to Constance. "Split up. Divide and conquer. Sounds good, eh?"

Constance apparently agreed with this suggestion, because she immediately streaked off in another direction. To Jack's displeasure, all three pirates kept chasing him. Not one of them ran after Constance! Not even Louis. Jack guessed the pirate's thirst for vengeance wasn't as strong as his hunger for power.

As Jack skidded around one corner, he made a quick mental note of where he was—looked like the town mill, right there—and prepared to keep running. But then he heard a loud whisper: "Jack!"

He wheeled about to see Arabella and Fitzwilliam, both of them peering through the bottom of one of the mill's windows.

They'd taken refuge in a corner and invited Jack to join them.

"Don't mind if I do," he muttered.

Fitzwilliam and Arabella were hiding behind barrels of grain stacked in one corner of the mill, opposite from the mill wheel and grindstone. Everything smelled of wheat and barley, scents Jack associated more strongly with ale than with bread.

"Thank goodness it's ye!" Arabella said. "We heard rustle in the brush and thought the worst. We thought it was pirates."

"This proves," Jack said, ducking down beside them and breathing heavily, "that you should always go with your initial instinct."

"You mean—" Fitzwilliam began.

"They were right on my tail, in fact. Two pirates and Captain Louis himself. But I seem to have lost them in the brush, thanks to my expert maneuvering."

"Ha. Thanks to *our* saving you!" Fitzwilliam scoffed.

"Whatever you want to believe, mate. So, how did you two wind up here anyway? Shouldn't you be back at the dock by now?"

"Well," Fitzwilliam began, "first my golden watch was stolen."

"Stolen?" He stared at them both. "How did you manage to get anything *stolen* in a town with no people?"

"One person," Fitzwilliam interjected, holding up a gloved finger. "As it turns out, this is a town with one person."

"A *thief*," Arabella added. Then she set about explaining just why Puerto San Judas was deserted in the first place.

"I suppose we have to look on the bright side," Jack said at last. "We've all avoided Left-Foot Louis, we now know for certain that the Sword and the sheath—even separately—have certain unknown but intriguing powers. All we have to do is lie low, find a way to procure the parchment—"

"What is this about a parchment?" Fitzwilliam asked. "Whatever does a scrap of paper have to do with our situation?"

Jack shrugged. "I'm a mite unclear on that point myself, mate. But let's burn that bridge when we get to it, shall we?"

Fitzwilliam frowned. "I do not think that is the proper use of the metaphor."

"Oh, yes, this is a perfect time for an English lesson. Can we conjugate verbs next?" Jack said sarcastically.

At that moment, the door of the mill swung open, and Louis walked in. He'd found them after all! Jack, Arabella, and Fitzwilliam all ducked lower, their chins almost scraping the floor. They could hear several boots thumping on the mill's floor; Louis hadn't come alone.

"This must be my lucky day!" Louis's voice boomed. "The parchment is just up the hill, the Sword in my hands, the sheath so close I can smell it—"

Arabella and Fitzwilliam looked at Jack, concerned. Jack made a face at them, then angled his head between two barrels so that he could get a glimpse of what was going on in the mill. From the sounds of pushing and struggle, apparently some kind of a scuffle was taking place.

"—and best of all," Louis finished, "we have finally found our missing sailors."

The pirates laughed as the two grave-digging thugs dragged forward—Jean and Tumen! Jack's eyes grew wide.

"We aren't the sailors you're looking for!" Jean protested. His face was taut with fear,

but he shouted bravely at the pirates. "You're crazy, all of you!"

"Let us go," Tumen said, more quietly. If he was frightened, too—and surely he had to be—he did not show it. The pirate ignored Tumen and threw the boys to the ground. Then he tied their hands behind their backs.

Next to Jack, Arabella gasped. Fitzwilliam grabbed her hand, like *that* was going to help anything. Jack rolled his eyes.

Louis paced along the floor, his two left feet making each step irregular. "I could kill you both with just a wave of my blade," he said grimly, holding out the Sword of Cortés. Jack realized that the pirate could simply make his fellow adventurers vanish in the blink of an eye, just as he'd done to the rest of the town. "But," Louis continued, "you interfered with a heist before, and I promised that the second time you meddled in my plans—and that would be today, in case you're wondering—that you'd die slowly and painfully. And, after all—" He leaned close to Jean and Tumen's faces. "—I'm nothing if not a man of my word."

Jack sighed. "Well, I suppose this means a rescue is in order," he whispered.

"A rescue?" Fitzwilliam asked. "You can not mean that you intend to fight against three pirates? One of whom has a magical sword?

Jack winked, smiling at Fitzwilliam.

"You *are* mad," Fitzwilliam said.

Louis shouted, "First, I'll grind the insolent looks on your sweet little faces on the millstone. How does that sound?"

Jean and Tumen never got a chance to answer. At that moment, Jack leaped up from behind the barrels, holding the sheath tightly and brandishing a sword he swiped from Fitzwilliam, which was far stronger than his own. Looking every bit as terrifying, dangerous, and legendary as he could manage, Jack Sparrow prepared for battle.

CHAPTER SIX

*W*ith a roar, Left-Foot Louis lunged at Jack. Jack stepped nimbly out of the way and plunged back into the swordfight he'd run from not even an hour before. This time, he reasoned, gritting his teeth as he struggled to parry Louis's thrusts, he'd do better. Then, the blade of the Sword of Cortés slashed so close to Jack that the breeze tickled his ear.

"You'd have done better to run while you could, mongrel," Louis boomed. "This here

sword? It could turn you into so much as thin air on my word."

"No, it can't," Jack taunted. "Disappear me, and you disappear the sheath," Jack said, waving the sheath in front of Louis. "Then, guess what? No godlike power for poor Louis. Savvy?"

Louis froze at the thought that he might accidentally send both Jack and the sheath away with the next move he made. Jack smiled proudly.

Louis's dismay lasted only for a minute. "You're right—I can't vanish you." He slashed with the Sword again, this time cutting a button from Jack's coat. It clattered to the floor. "But the Sword of Cortés is still a sword. It can cut you to shreds just fine."

"Good point," Jack said. Another swipe of the blade came within inches of Jack's chest.

In the blur around him, he could see that Arabella was struggling to untie the ropes that bound Jean and Tumen. She looked likely to get them free at any moment. But where was Fitzwilliam?

And then Fitzwilliam appeared right between Jack and Louis. He quickly grabbed the sheath out of Jack's hand, held it up to the pirate captain, and smiled. When the pirate jabbed at him, Fitzwilliam grabbed his sword back from Jack, and the blade clashed with the Sword of Cortés so sharply that sparks flew. "Perhaps," Fitzwilliam said quietly, "you would prefer dueling an equal."

Louis laughed. "I would. But I'll have to make do with you."

Their battle began. Jack watched as the two of them began dueling, matching each other parry for parry, stroke for stroke. He was held in astonishment by the speed of the fight, at least until Arabella tugged at his sleeve. "Fitzwilliam helped ye, now help me!"

"Fitzy helped me? What help? I didn't need any help!" Jack said, annoyed.

"He saved ye, didn't he? Now help me cut through this knot!" Arabella barked.

"*Oui*, Jack," Jean said, sounding less cheerful than Jack had ever heard him before.

"Fitz? Saved my life!?" Jack had never heard anything so ridiculous. Still, he set about helping Arabella sever the last of the cords binding Jean and Tumen. "I didn't need saving!"

"Is that why your clothing is cut to ribbons?" Jean asked.

"Hardly ribbons. A tear. Maybe two."

Tumen tossed the sliced ropes from his wrists. "Maybe ten or twelve," he said.

"I didn't need saving!" Jack repeated.

The clash of metal drew his attention

back to the fight between Left-Foot Louis and Fitzwilliam P. Dalton III. Despite Louis's being podiatrically challenged, he was a powerful sword fighter—quick with his blade, strong with his strokes. But—to Jack's amazement—Fitzwilliam was even better. He could parry every blow and predict all of Louis's moves.

Must be that fancy training of his, Jack thought.

"Jack!" Arabella called out to him.

Jack looked to his left, and there was one of Louis's angry pirate thugs. He looked quickly to his right, and there was the other. Jack stood between them. "Come and get me, mates!" The pirates lunged forward at the same time, and Jack quickly jumped up and grabbed onto a low-hanging rafter. The two pirates collided and fell to the ground. Jack dropped back down and kicked them hard in their heads with the soles of his boots, knocking them unconscious. "That was easy," he said, smiling.

Behind Jack, the battle between Louis and Fitzwilliam was raging. Louis suddenly surprised Fitzwilliam by lunging forward and slashing the Sword of Cortés down hard. Fitzwilliam almost got himself out of the way, so he survived the blow—but the tip of the blade cut deeply into his arm. Fitzwilliam shouted in pain. The sheath flew from his hand, and Jack lunged forward and grabbed it once more.

"See there?" Jack said proudly. "I told you. Who is the one among us who needs saving now?" He stepped over the unconscious thugs and picked up a large bag of flour. "Watch and learn. I'm about to save Fitzy's life. And do you think anyone will notice? No. Of course not." Jack swung the bag of flour, hard, smack into Louis's face. A cloud of white billowed out around them as the pirate staggered back three steps, then fell, stunned, to the floor.

This was good. The fact that the pirate had dropped the Sword of Cortés—even better!

Jack grabbed the Sword before Left-Foot Louis could gather his wits. Jack had his old, rusty sword in one hand and the shiniest magical sword he had ever seen in the other. This was more like it. He pointed both swords at the pirate and said, "Seems high time for some surrender."

Fitzwilliam, panting for breath after his fight, wrapped a handkerchief around his bleeding arm. Though he was exhausted, no serious damage had been done. Tumen was rather matter-of-factly tying up the two unconscious pirates, so as to avoid any trouble when they woke up again. Jean's curly hair, messed by his struggle, stuck out in all directions, making him look crazy as he held his knife toward Louis as an additional warning. Every single one of the boys was grinning like mad.

But Arabella wasn't smiling.

"You," she said.

"That's right." Jack straightened up proudly. "Me. The one who *saved* Fitz. Not the other way around."

"I could have rallied," Fitzwilliam said.

"Not likely," Jack replied.

Arabella just whispered it again, "You." Her voice shook with loathing, which tipped Jack off to the fact that she wasn't talking to him at all. Instead, she was staring at Left-Foot Louis, her hands bunched into fists. "Do you remember me?"

"You're a bit young for my taste, lass,"

Louis jeered. "Not to mention a bit scrawny. And a bit dirty."

"Be silent!" Fitzwilliam demanded. "You will not insult this lady."

Jack looked back and forth between Arabella and the pirate. He couldn't quite figure out what was happening—but events had definitely taken a turn for the weird. Why had Arabella not revealed her connection—whatever it may be—to Louis before?

"Don't bother lecturing him, Fitz," Arabella said. "He'll never learn. He'll never have the time." She grabbed the Sword of Cortés from Jack, moving so quickly that Jack didn't even realize what she was doing until the blade was in her hands. She looked angrier than ever with the Sword in her hand. Jack and the crew had never seen her like this before. It was as if she had become a dark shadow of herself.

In two quick strides, Arabella was standing over Left-Foot Louis. To Jack's shock, she pressed the tip of the blade to Louis's throat.

"Pirate!" Arabella ground out between her clenched teeth. "Ye killed me mother!"

CHAPTER SEVEN

$\mathcal{J}$ack couldn't take his eyes from Arabella's face. She was filled with rage—angrier than anyone Jack had ever seen, angrier even than the legendary Captain Torrents, whose rage could stir a hurricane.* Her eyes brimmed with angry tears. Fitzwilliam took a step closer to her. "Arabella—"

But Louis cut him off. "Ah, I do know

---

*As Jack and his crew learned the hard way in Vol. 1: *The Coming Storm* where I have seen you before," he said to Arabella. "Tortuga. Seems I remember a loud-mouthed wench and her miserable little brat. Shut that wench's mouth, I did. Too bad I didn't shut yours."

"I'll kill ye!" Arabella's whole body shook with rage, but her grip on the Sword remained firm. "I will kill ye dead, ye filthy, miserable pirate."

None of the *Barnacle*'s crew doubted that Arabella meant what she said. Within a few moments, Louis would be dead on the floor, and Arabella would be a killer. Jack had no doubt of that. He had never thought of Arabella as the murderous type, but then, he'd never known that her mother had been killed by this particular big, mean—not to mention ugly—pirate. The anger in her was something she'd been saving up ever since her mother died. Soon it would turn

Arabella into someone Jack was certain she didn't want to be.

Jack made a grab for the Sword of Cortés, but Arabella elbowed him in the ribs so that he staggered to one side. "Ye can have the Sword later, Jack!" she shouted. "But not now. Not yet."

"Look, lass. Let's think about this a moment," Jack said flatly. "What say we tie him up for now, hmm? You can think it over. Plenty of time to get rid of him for good later, if you're still in the mood. The day's still young."

"She will do *nothing* to me." Louis barked, seeming much too confident for a man who had a sword at his throat—a legendary, magical sword no less. "Haven't got the nerve for it, have you, pretty?"

Arabella had the nerve for it; of that Jack had no doubt. As she leaned forward, pressing the blade's point ever more sharply against the pirate's throat, Louis's smug grin began to fade.

"Arabella, no," Tumen whispered, but she paid him no mind. Behind him, Fitzwilliam and Jean stared, their mouths agape in shock.

"I've waited so long for this," she said. It sounded as though she might burst into tears. "Ye can't know how I've waited. Because ye can't know what it's like to lose someone you love. A pirate can love no one."

"Bell, let's try this again. Take a step back here and reconsider, eh?" Jack stepped closer to her, friendly-like, wondering how near he'd have to be to successfully swipe the sword from her. "Remember all that Fitzy here was saying about the law in these parts? Be a shame to deprive them of the hanging of a pirate, wouldn't you say?"

"Why are ye trying to stop me?" Arabella

cried out. "Ye hate him as much as I do! Why do ye want to save him? Everyone *back away* from me! Now!"

The Sword of Cortés glowed. It was as if the air around the crew shivered and turned warm, rippling like a tide pool stirred by the breeze. Jack, Fitz, Jean, and Tumen all staggered backward, as if pushed—but the force moving them was completely invisible. Jean actually tumbled down until his back thudded against the wall of the mill. By the time any of them could stop skidding, they were all at least several feet from Arabella and Louis. Jack's eyes grew wide in wonder at the Sword's magic. And that magic belonged to Arabella as long as she held Cortés's blade. How much *more* powerful could a Sword like that *become*?

"Listen to me," Jack said gently. "Bell, put the Sword away."

"Don't call me 'Bell,'" Arabella said. Then, in a more sober voice, she continued, "You only call me that when you want something."

"I call you that because I know you. I know what sort of person you are. You wouldn't kill someone in cold blood. Not like this."

"That's how he killed my mother. In cold blood."

"And that's why you're not going to kill him. Because you're better than he is." Jack tried taking a step toward her. The Sword's magic didn't push him back, and Arabella didn't protest. Her arm was trembling now, and her gaze was fixed on the Sword, pressed against Louis's neck.

Left-Foot Louis was terrified now, whether of the magic, Arabella, or both, no one knew.

"Her name was Laura," she whispered.

"She was so beautiful and so *good*. Ye remember it, do ye?" Arabella's voice shook again. "That night at the tavern—ye tried putting an arm around her, and she'd have none of it. So ye grabbed her by her hair and called her names—when me dad tried to stop ye, the thugs from the *Cutlass* stopped him. Broke his bones. And ye left me to watch while ye dragged her outside. None of us ever saw her again. I didn't even get to say good-bye."

"Bell," Jack murmured. He wasn't trying to get her attention; he only wanted her to remember that her friends were there beside her.

"After she was gone, I had to do me mum's job at the Faithful Bride, with drunken sailors cursing at me all day and all night. Me dad drank too much before she died, and after—there was nothing left of

him. When the tavern closed each night, I had to clean up after all the drunken fools and then clean up after Dad, too. He was a good father—once—he was—" Tears were welling in Arabella's eyes again.

"Ye as much as killed him, too, when ye took me mum. All that time, I've been alone. And all that time, I've known who took my family away. But I look at ye now and—killing ye won't bring Mum back." She slumped, as if defeated.

"Bell," Jack said, "put the Sword away. We're not like him. We're not killers. We're not pirates."

Arabella stumbled backward, just two steps. Her hand gripped the sword so tightly that her knuckles grew white. The great struggle within her heart showed on her face. Slowly, so slowly that it took Jack a moment to realize she was moving, Arabella let her arm fall to her side. Then she breathed out a hard sigh of disappointment and release. It was over.

Louis sat up. "I told you that you wouldn't—" he said.

His sneering words were cut off by Fitzwilliam, who kicked Louis squarely in the jaw.

Arabella's cheeks were bright with tears, but she didn't give in to crying. Her eyes were feverish and somewhat wild. If she were the sort of girl to burst into sobs and Jack were the sort of boy to comfort a crying girl—well, Jack thought, they might have done something like that. But she kept her glare fixed on Louis as the others bound him up tightly with rope.

"He will go to jail," Fitzwilliam said reassuringly. "Undoubtedly he will be hanged, in accordance with the law. The *Cutlass* will be cut up into kindling and sent to Pirate Cove, and no one will again suffer because of Louis's cruelty. Not ever again, Arabella. All because of you."

"Until they hang ye," Arabella said to Louis, "I will hate ye, every day. And after the hanging, maybe I'll have some peace." She laughed, a strange, broken sound. "My great—my *only*—wish is that my mother may find you, wherever she may be—in this world, the next, or anywhere in between. May justice be done. And let it be done by *her* hand."

The Sword of Cortés began to glow again, and everyone in the mill knew what was happening. The air rippled as it had before. And Louis writhed and howled . . . then vanished.

Jean said something in French that Jack suspected wasn't very polite. Tumen looked around wildly. Fitzwilliam stamped his foot upon the place where Louis had been, but his buckled shoe hit only the floor.

Jack realized it was all over. Left-Foot Louis had disappeared—for good.

CHAPTER EIGHT

For a few long moments, the crew of the *Barnacle* stared at Arabella in horrified fascination.

"Impossible," Arabella whispered, gazing at the still-glowing sword in her hand.

"Amazing, isn't it, how many impossible things are nonetheless true?" Jack folded his arms and studied the empty spot where Left-Foot Louis used to be.

"The Sword of Cortés did this,"

Fitzwilliam said, leaving Jack to wonder why Fitz always needed to state the obvious. "You wished that justice might be done by your mother's hand, and then he disappeared."

Tumen kept staring suspiciously around the mill. "Her mother is dead. So where did the pirate go?"

"The afterlife," Jean said, as though it were obvious. "He took the ropes with him, so he's still tied up, wherever he is. I hope he stays tied up forever, Arabella."

"I killed him." Arabella tossed the Sword of Cortés to the mill floor, where it clattered against the wood, and then held her hands up to her quivering mouth. Fitzwilliam took one step toward Arabella and made an attempt to touch her shoulder, but she jerked away from him. "I killed him, just the same as if I'd cut his throat."

"Oh, no, you didn't!" Jack protested. Then it occurred to him that he didn't know that, exactly. "It doesn't count if you didn't *mean* to kill him. It's a rule somewhere. In some sort of code or rule book somewhere. Really. I'm sure of it."

Tumen looked skeptical. "I'm not sure that's true."

Jack frantically waved off this objection. "Besides, Louis could still be alive!"

"Alive?" Arabella said. "Yes, if you consider somewhere in the afterlife alive. But it does seem like a pretty dead type of being alive to me." Arabella was now shivering violently, as though she were freezing instead of sweating in the heat of the warm Caribbean afternoon.

Jean shrugged. "He could be alive. Stranger things have happened, right?"

"I don't think so," Tumen said.

"But it's possible!" Jean was grinning now. "We know these things, in Creole lands. The living and the dead aren't as separate as you think. Haven't you heard of a zombie before?"

Arabella went pale. Fitzwilliam said, "If we could refrain from speaking about zombies, I think that would be best."

"Not helping a bit," Jack agreed. "But I meant what I said. There is a great possibility that Left-Foot Louis is still alive."

"How do you know?" Tumen asked.

"Because—think of what Arabella said last. Right before Louis did that spiffy vanishing thing. She said, 'May justice be done.' What does that sound like to you, eh?"

"Justice. You mean—the law?" Arabella sounded a little more hopeful. "The Sword might have sent him to a jail somewhere?"

Jack felt encouraged. In truth, he didn't

have the slightest idea where Louis had gone, and he didn't much care, either. The main thing was that Louis was gone. And the second-to-main thing was getting his first mate back into shipshape condition.

"Exactly. Precisely. Jail," Jack continued. "Probably dropped Left-Foot Louis right in front of the closest magistrate, just like you wanted. Not too shabby."

"She also said that she wanted justice to be done by her mother's hand," Tumen reminded Jack.

Arabella wilted again, and Jack scowled at Tumen.

"Look here—did you ever hear of the figurative sense of things?" Jack said. "Fitz here could fill you in, I am sure, what with all his correcting of people's English and such. Justice is served by her mother's hand, symbolically."

"That's right. Must be." Arabella took a deep breath, clearly trying to convince herself that this was the truth. "Just give me a moment."

Everyone kept a respectful silence—for Arabella's sake, not for the memory of the worthless Left-Foot Louis. She turned toward the corner, hugging herself, and Jack thought it wisest to leave her alone for a bit.

Then Jean, having a moment to gather his thoughts and his composure, suddenly snapped, "Constance! Where is she?"

That blasted cat! Jack had almost forgotten about that poor excuse for an old floor mat. "She was with me up at the church, where we ran into Left-Foot Louis in the first place."

Jean flinched. "But no! He hated Constance! Tell me he didn't hurt her. Did he? Are you just trying to find a way to break it to me gently?"

"Your strange cat-sister-beastie-thing is in the pink of health," Jack said. "So far as I know," he continued. "At least she was the last time I saw her."

Jean glared at Jack. "The last time you *saw* her?" he shouted, panicked.

"Calm down, calm down," Jack replied. "She ran off not long after the fighting started. As far as I know, she's somewhere between here and there. Wherever there might be," Jack said.

"Jack!" Jean snapped, flustered.

"They were last up by the church, now we are at the mill," Fitzwilliam said, placing a hand on Jean's shoulder. "We have a path to follow, then." Fitzwilliam was speaking calmly, as if he were sure they'd find Constance easily, but also like he didn't care if they never saw the cat again. "Shall we take a walk toward the church? I believe fresh air might prove bracing."

"All right," Arabella said, clearly gathering herself together. "Let's go."

Just then, one of the pirate thugs lying on the floor sat up and looked around in a daze. "Captain!" he bellowed. "Where is our Captain, Louis? What have you lot of curs done with him?"

Jack considered how best to answer this, then picked up the Sword of Cortés and smashed the hilt down on the pirate's head. The pirate fell down, unconscious again. "Right, that's taken care of," Jack said.

Casually, hoping no one would take notice, Jack slipped the Sword into its sheath—uniting these two parts for the first time in a long while, making them whole again. He half-expected the room to ripple with magic, or a shower of sparks and light, or something else of a dazzling nature. Instead, the Sword fell into place like any other sword in any other sheath. Obviously, that parchment was the key piece of the puzzle. Jack would need that before he could do anything really impressive. But he still didn't know exactly what this parchment was.

The crew walked up the hill under the hot afternoon sun. Nobody spoke. They were all aware, however, that they'd taken care of only three out of the many pirates aboard the *Cutlass*. Left-Foot Louis might be in jail, or a zombie, or whatever else the Sword of Cortés had seen fit to do with him, but there was still a whole crew of pirates who could cause a lot of trouble. Fortunately, Jack and his crew were able to make their way to the church without seeing any sign of them.

As they walked through the front

doors, Fitzwilliam broke the silence. "What were pirates doing in a church? I would wager they were not there to offer alms."

"Oh, they were just doing some grave-robbing," Jack replied with relish. "Digging up old bones, that sort of thing. Typical pirate happenings."

Tumen made a face. "Disgusting."

"Horrible," Arabella said, shuddering.

Jean grinned. "Constance!"

Jean ran out the church's back door. There, atop the coffin the pirates had unearthed, lay Constance—sleeping in a sunbeam that fell along the casket lid.

"My beautiful sister!" Jean cuddled the cat against his chest; Constance blinked drowsily and looked as though she would much rather have been left to her nap. "You're safe, thank goodness."

"Beautiful?" Jack asked.

"Sleeping on a coffin?" Arabella folded her arms and looked quite cross. "Honestly, Constance. How gruesome of ye."

Constance licked her ragged whiskers, unconcerned. Arabella shook her head in exasperation.

"Left-Foot Louis was rather interested in this here coffin." Jack said. "Specifically, the man inside the coffin, once known as Francois, may he rest in peace. After today, I mean."

The crew looked over at the coffin, which Louis's men had already opened part of the way.

"Yuck," Jean said.

"What did he want with Francois's body?" Fitzwilliam asked.

"Well, even more specifically, he wanted a bit of parchment this Francois had on his person when he shuffled off to wherever it is dead people shuffle off to," Jack replied.

99

"This parchment. The one ye mentioned before. What's so important about it?" Arabella peered down suspiciously at the coffin and shivered at the sight of the decomposing corpse. The afternoon breeze ruffled her messy hair.

Jack put his hands behind his back and rocked back and forth, smiling. "Seems to have something to do with the Sword of Cortés."

"A treasure map to its location? But Louis had already found the Sword, in Stone-Eyed Sam's throne room."* Fitzwilliam gestured at the sword and sheath at Jack's side. "You already have the scabbard. Therefore, the parchment can be of no use to us. That sword at your side, Jack, it is already imbued with godlike power!"

"No, it is not. Not yet," Jack said flatly.

*Back in Vol. i: *The Coming Storm*

The *Barnacle*'s crew looked confused.

Jack continued, "Seems that this parchment has the ability to unlock the true—the full—power of the Sword of Cortés."

"Oh, no." Arabella shook her head, as if she were really thinking about this for the very first time. "Jack, that sword's power is already huge. It's already dangerous."

"Very true. So how could the parchment make it any *worse*?" Smiling hopefully, Jack gestured toward the coffin.

"I agree with Arabella," Tumen said, stepping back to put distance between him and Jack. "The Sword has hurt many people. It should not hurt any more."

"Don't look at me." Jean clutched Constance tighter. "I don't care one way or the other about the Sword, but messing with that dead body in there? Yuck! Not for me."

To Jack's surprise, Fitzwilliam stepped

forward. "Jack is right. We must obtain the parchment."

Everyone stared at him. Jack was the first to find his voice. "Although I am of course surprised and delighted to hear you making sense for once, Fitzy—what on earth has brought you around to my side?"

"Let us consider this closely," Fitzwilliam said, speaking to everyone but Jack. "If Left-Foot Louis knew the parchment was here, chances are that others do as well. Anyone who later finds this parchment will then come after the Sword—and after those who *possess* it. In other words, they will come after *us*. But if this grave is dug up again in the future, and if those who do it do not find the parchment because we have taken it, they will think the stories to be untrue. They will not come after the Sword, they will not come after us, and we will remain safe. At the very least, this parchment must be retrieved and safely hidden."

Arabella wasn't convinced. She was wringing her hands together, nervous and uneasy. "We could drop the Sword off the side of the *Barnacle*. In fact, we should. Let it fall to the bottom of the sea, where it belongs."

"Oh, yes, 'where it belongs'—with Davy Jones, the Sirens and the merfolk, and who knows what else?" Jack said. "We know now the sea is no safer a place than the land."

The crew nodded in agreement.

Jack decided it might be time to add his perspective, too. "Besides, after all we've been through—Bell, aren't you just a little curious?" She raised an eyebrow, studying him. "All those sailors' tales you've listened to. All the legends you drank in while the pirates were gulping their ale at the Faithful

Bride. Don't you want to know if they're true? Aren't you ready to see for yourself? And, think for a moment, all of you, of the type of freedom such power would bestow upon us."

Arabella hesitated—and then she and Jack shared a deliciously happy smile. "Well then, I gather it's as good a day as any to become a grave robber," she said. After a moment, Jean and Tumen nodded their consent as well.

It took both Fitzwilliam and Jack to remove the rest of the coffin lid. The iron hinges had rusted right off, though most of the wood was still heavy and strong. Finally, Fitzwilliam put his shoulder into it, and the lid swung all the way back. Francois's skeleton was dressed in regal clothing. His dusty gray skull grinned at the crew. Tumen shuddered, and Fitzwilliam winced from the moldy smell. Even Jack didn't like the look of the thing.

And there, in the pocket of the skeleton's elegant waistcoat, Jack found the parchment they'd been seeking.

CHAPTER NINE

"What have we here?" Jack whispered, leaning over Francois's remains. Carefully, he tugged the parchment from the skeleton's coat. The sheet fluttered free, and Arabella quickly pushed the lid of the coffin shut again.

"The parchment," Jean whispered. "It unlocks the godlike power of the Sword?"

"So they say." Jack grinned.

"Now you have the parchment. Do you have godlike power already?" Tumen asked.

Jack considered this for a moment. "Don't think so." He put his hand on the Sword. "No tingling, no humming, nothing special." He looked up at the sunny sky and made a swirling gesture with his hand as if he were trying to stir up clouds, but no rain began to fall. "Nope. Definitely not godlike."

"Perhaps merely possessing the parchment is not enough," Fitzwilliam pointed out. "Perhaps there is some sort of magic spell or incantation written upon it."

"Of course there's an incantation written upon it. I was just waiting to see how long it would take you all to realize it," Jack said.

Jack smoothed the parchment out atop the lid of Francois's coffin. Sure enough, something was written on it, in ink so old that it had faded to mere scratches of sepia. "Can't quite make this out," Jack muttered as he squinted at it.

Arabella seemed distracted, "We really ought to bury Francois. Rebury him, I mean."

"Wait," Jack said holding his arm out as if he were stopping Arabella. Grinning, he added, "It'll be a lot easier to lower him down and shovel dirt over him once we have godlike power."

Fitzwilliam leaned next to Jack to study the parchment for himself. "I do not believe that this is written in English."

"Spanish, I could figure out," Jack said, "but it's not Spanish. That would just be too bloody convenient, wouldn't it?"

"It's not French or Creole, either," Jean offered. "Tumen, does this look like your tribe's language?"

Tumen shook his head and said, "I have never seen anything like this." Arabella shrugged, too.

Jack studied Fitzwilliam's face. "You're not saying something, Fitz. Out with it."

"Ah. Yes. Well." Fitzwilliam glanced first in one direction, then in another, as if looking for rescue that did not come. His cheeks were turning red. "I think that this is written in Latin."

"Latin! Fitz, that's perfect!" Arabella brightened. "Ye learned Latin from your tutors! I remember when ye told us of all the languages you speak." *

Jack's face lit up. "Thank everything blessed and cursed that you aristos learn all those bloody dead languages!" he said.

Tugging at his collar, Fitzwilliam said, "I fear I must admit that I was not always the most attentive of pupils for my Latin tutor."

Constance cocked her head, as though

---

*Fitz did, in fact, tell them he spoke Latin, see Vol. 1: *The Coming Storm* for proof!

puzzled. Jean stroked her fur as he asked, "What is that supposed to mean?"

"It means Fitzy here doesn't speak a word of Latin." Jack couldn't believe it. "The *only* useful thing you could've absorbed in your high-and-mighty education, and you didn't learn it. Absolutely brilliant."

Fitzwilliam straightened up, reasserting his dignity. "I submit to you that I could scarcely have known that I would need Latin to decipher a magical scroll granting godlike power to the bearer of the Sword of Cortés."

"Oh, you've no imagination at all," Jack said dismissively.

"But—then—" looking bewildered, Arabella asked Fitz, "why did ye say ye spoke Latin when ye didn't?"

Jack was the one who answered her. "Some lads just can't resist showing off for the lasses. And usually it's the lads with the least to brag about." Fitz's face grew red with anger, and Jack wondered if he was about to see Fitzwilliam lose his temper again. The aristocrat's fits of rage were always fun for some sparring practice.

Arabella stepped between them, clearly eager to make the peace. "Fitz, how much did you learn? Anything?"

"A few words. Pronunciation. No more."

To Jack's surprise, Arabella nodded with satisfaction. "Well, then, that's all ye need. As long as ye read it aloud correctly, the incantation should work. Ye don't have to understand what it says."

"Wait," Tumen interrupted. "We would be calling forth great magical power without knowing precisely what we are doing. Don't you think this might be unwise?"

"We've never known what we were doing

111

before," Jack reminded him. "Why should we let that stop us now?"

"But Tumen surely has a point," Fitzwilliam said.

Jack snatched up the parchment from the coffin lid. "If you were all a bunch of scaredy-cats—and please feel free to take offense to that, Constance—why did you help me get the parchment in the first place? You've just lost your nerve, the lot of you. We've come this far. Let's finish. Let's use the Sword of Cortés."

Slowly, Arabella nodded. Tumen sighed, but he did not say anything else. Jean nodded gamely. Fitzwilliam was the last of them to agree, but he finally cleared his throat and said, "I am ready."

"I've got the Sword, and it's in its sheath," Jack said, checking at his side to make sure nothing magical had happened to either item, but they were right there where they belonged and seemed as normal as ever. "I should be holding the parchment, too. You read it off, Fitz, and I'll repeat after you. Got it?"

"Aye, 'Captain,'" Fitzwilliam said, saluting dramatically and leaning over Jack's shoulder.

The breeze stirred everyone's hair. The empty town of Puerto San Judas had never sounded as silent as it did that moment. Even the birds seemed to have stopped singing. Everybody crowded closer to Jack and Fitzwilliam as Fitzwilliam began to read aloud:

"*Poena Letum Pugna.*"

Jack repeated, loudly and proudly, "*Poena Letum Pugna!*"

"Did he say 'pain?'" Jean whispered to Tumen. Jack pretended not to hear.

Fitzwilliam said, "*Envinco*—"

"*Envinco.*"

"*Inhumanus.*"

"*Inhumanus!*" Jack finished, shouting it out, to make sure the godlike power knew to come to *him* instead of Fitz.

Silence. Nobody moved. Jack waited for any of the humming, tingling, or glowing that ought to accompany godlike power. None developed.

"Is that all?" Jack said, turning the parchment over in case something else was written on the back. But the other side was blank.

Arabella scratched her head. "The change must not be obvious. Try to do something magical."

Jack did the first thing that came to mind. He pointed at Constance and said, "Turn this thing back into Jean's sister!"

Constance mewed once, then began washing herself with her paw. Jean slumped in disappointment. "Why didn't it work?"

"Maybe because she was never a girl to begin with, lad," Jack said, patting Jean on the head.

"Any idea at all what this says in English?" Jack asked Fitzwilliam.

Fitz shook his head.

"At all?"

Fitz shrugged.

"Just a little? A word or two?"

"No!" Fitzwilliam yelled out.

"Okay, no need to go mad over it."

Jack put his hand beneath his chin and considered the Sword. Clearly another test was needed, but what?

"Aha!" he said, then lifted the Sword high in the air and commanded, "Bring all the citizens of Puerto San Judas back home!"

Again, silence. No one filled the church. No people wandered the roads.

Fitzwilliam said, "Possibly no one was attending church at the time."

Tumen shook his head. "Incense is still burning. They were here, but they haven't come back."

"It didn't work," Arabella said, disappointed.

"Didn't work?" Jack stared down at the sword at his side. "What do you mean, it didn't work? You don't go finding a magical sword *and* a magical sheath *and* a secret incantation, and then just have it—not work! And, besides . . ." Jack began, "it worked before! Why now, when it's in its sheath where it is supposed to be, is it not working? I blame you, Fitz," Jack said dismissively. "Your pronunciation was all wrong. I'm sure of it. Positive, in fact."

"I can't believe it," Arabella said. "It makes no sense at all."

"Blasted pirate stories." Jack could have pitched the sword and never looked back. He threw his hands up in the air in disgust and said, "Right. I'm headed back into the city to see if anyone left supper on. Coming?"

He turned to go—and that's when he saw the phantom. It wore a conquistador's armor, made of iron and silver, glowing slightly with heat. Steam and foul-smelling sulfur oozed from the bearded phantom's ears, mouth, and nostrils.

The phantom took one step toward them, its hellish armor clanking. Its eyes were red, and its beard curled like smoke. As the crew of the *Barnacle* all huddled close together, terrified, the phantom raised a hand and groaned in a gravely voice.

Arabella clutched Fitzwilliam's arm.

"Jack, don't ye realize what's happened? The pirates' stories lacked a wee detail! The incantation brought back the Sword's owner! This is the spirit of Hernán Cortés, risen from the dead!"

Cortés took one more step toward them, his glowing red eyes still fixed on the Sword. Nobody said a word. They were all too scared to speak—in fact, scared out of their wits.

Almost all of them, that is.

Jack took a jaunty step forward and extended his hand toward the conquistador. "Well, hello there, mate," he said. "Captain Jack Sparrow. How very nice to meet you."

To be concluded . . .

Don't miss the next volume in the continuing adventures of Jack Sparrow and the crew of the mighty Barnacle!

The Sword of Cortés

*J*ack Sparrow has the Sword of Cortés in hand. Godlike power will soon be his—but at what price? Featuring the corrosive conquistador, Cortés, himself, and the return of some very scaly antagonists. All this, plus a Caribbean snowfall. You wouldn't want to miss that, now, would you?